Parallel intersection

Rick Sandman

Contents

Prologue

Avantika's Pov:

The day was going as usual, just college events that made me feel alive. I would just want college to be the place where I can learn lots of new things.

Things were getting difficult, I couldn't breathe. The day was on loop again. That night, the following day, he was there, he wanted to do it.... I woke up in the middle of the night. I checked my phone, it was 3:00 am in the morning. The sky looked peaceful, though there was darkness it was my comfort place. The nightmare had always troubled me, but to my surprise it occurred after 2 months. I was alarmed by the strange return of the nightmare. But soon I just fell asleep.

The next morning was no different. I woke up for the lectures and spent some of my useful time reading the favorite novel of mine, "ME BEFORE YOU, by Jojo Moyes". It's one of a kind novel. I had fallen in love with books way before I actually fell in love with someone.

Love, it's a strange term. For some people it may be just a chemical reaction but to some it could mean so much more. For me the definition of love was always more. Love reminds of the poem I had once written.

Red roses and balloons,Is another perception;The serene feeling,Getting clumsy but prudent;Cherishing moments,Yet being dolorous;Worth being for,Also feeling futile.

Love enlocks,The door to yourself;Stops remorseing;Causes redemption;Untangles the tangles;And makes you!

Love is just subjective and for me it has always been simple. For being brought up in a brown household, I never thought something like love could ever happen to me. It was all just books that made me believe that for everyone there is a soulmate. Books made me fall in love with the authors, who would hype the narrative of love.All I wish was college being a place I glow.

Kanan's Pov :

I had the best day of my life. I was playing PS with Tej and samay, I finally won 5 out of 6 matches. And then we did our usual routine, went out to eat and look at some of the girls (a guy like me can only look at a girl but never talk to her). Each one of them is pretty in their own special way.Then i bid my goodbyes for the day and went home only to see mom had made my favourite food. She is one of the rare cool moms any guy could have had.She tells me I should get a girlfriend and go out more often.

When I was going to sleep I started thinking what if someday I find a girl who would be just perfect for herself, someone who knows her dark and bright side and would walk hell for me, someone I would want to change my whole world for, well I am getting ahead of myself. Love is a beautiful feeling and yet most disturbing one. Few months back I thought I would never meet the one but I guess I will someday.I am all for big romances but all I need now is My other half, my soulmate, my partner and my best friend.Well Kanan, enough of imagination to yourself let's go to sleep, we have got a big day.

Chapter 1

F INDINGS OF PAST

Avantika Pov :

A was sitting near my window, wondering how strange life has become. I had been in a relationship only for about 1year and one fine day he just texted me, " I know, you love me but I don't think this would work". I didn't know what to reply. It was during the time of the cyclone, there was no electricity. It was past 12:00 am. I just didn't know what I did wrong to make it fail. Sometimes, life gives you situations where even you don't know if this won't work what else would. Probably this is one of these scenes.

The following morning, my health deteriorated. I heard mom calling me," Avanti wakeup, it's past your bedtime."This moment was everything, I had no energy to get out of bed and carry on with chores. Yesterday night even the inside got all wet. The tears hadn't dried up, it was evident. The chest was all burdened with a new type of fear and failure.

Later on he called, maybe a sympathetic call. But for what I knew it was to make me feel guilty.He said," Whatever had happened was because I didn't want to hurt you, but you never understood so I had to put an end to this. We can stay in touch and I am there for you." After a long minute,he spoke again. "Avantika, you have to say something, this is what you always do. You never understand, you always want to just wait for things to happen." At this moment I decided to speak. "I thought you had called to apologize. But here again you and your nasty blame games." "Avanti, please not again. I just wanted to make sure, you are holding up well. You know this is all hard for me also." I said while sobbing,"If it is hard why do you want to give up Moksh, You love me don't you? You never really cared and now also as usual you want to break it cause, it wasn't helping you to get over your so-called love...."He angrily replied," Avantika just mind your language, just because I dated you doesn't give you the right to talk about her. I don't even know why I dated you. You always want to have fights and never understand. Never call or text me again. I called you to check on you, I do care about you Avanti." and then he just cut the call.

I tried calling him, but it seems like my tears never worked for him. I tried to call him a lot of times, but he won't pick up. I tried texting him. He didn't reply to me immediately. But then when he did it just broke my heart into a million pieces. I was used to getting hurt, because I guess my roots to valuing things made me weak and strong.

Well for me, this message was a pain? I couldn't explain or feel anything. My eyes wanted to read something that would just make me forget " I never had any love feelings for you", so I decided to read a note he had written to me in the past week. The note went like,

Avantika is my avanti , when I cry she wipes it, when I do some shit in my life she is there to wipe it, I don't about true love, and I know I am too weak or bad at expressing love, but I gotta say I love you Avanti very much and also that I know you will never ever leave me under any condition I believe even I won't leave you. We have some special kind of bond right now, I don't know what kind of bond but whatever it is, we call it love and I love it and u too. I just wanna say I'm gonna be there for you forever, and sorry I become jealous sometimes, coz I love you, you have only right over me, no one else so shut the fuck up and don't see anyone else and yeah I'm sorry I get angry quickly, but still I would continue loving you again.

This was my comfort place. This has been a part of me for a long period of time.

Suddenly, I was remembering all the moments I had spent with him. It's weird at the moment those happy moments were always torturing the soul of mine.

Mom called me, I had to answer because without that I would have surely made my already worse day, worst.

She asked me if i could walk to the grocery shop and I needed that so bad. Maybe a walk could make me feel better, so I said yes I will go.

Only if I knew that I would have to take help of walks to gain my sanity back, would I have done a long back.

After I came back home, I felt nothing. I always knew this was going to happen. Regardless of his repetitive mistakes, physical and mental torture I just hoped that he would turn into the man I wanted him to be. But the irony is he turned me into the woman he wanted and I hated.

It was the journey of all fire walks, but I knew I was ice and had to melt so I could put off the fire for myself.

That night I lost a younger version of myself and created a version that little Avanti wanted for like an eternity.

I was happy with him, the way he used to understand me was quite different. People maybe that's why saying love makes you feel different.

I told myself "I won't be in love until someone makes me believe in love again.Until someone who never promises but always shows up, someone who values me as a person and never ever makes me feel I was a rebound again".

Memories with Moksh still haunt me especially the incident when......, I was lost in the thoughts when dad called me.

Thank you so much for reading Let me know what you guys think of Moksh and what was the incident she was talking!!!!

Lots of love,Avantika

Chapter 2

H^{er}

I saw her for the first time. She is the definition of beauty. Anyone who looked at her would be in love with her smile, the way she smiles makes everyone around her happy. I was day dreaming about her again, but I can't help but think about her.

"I will tell you how I saw her for the first time." I say to Tej.

"Remember Tej, when we had gone to get prints?" I ask him.

"Yes" he said plainly

"I was standing in the queue, I was looking around seeing my dream college when I saw her, she looks like my dream.She was walking next to me in her beautiful brown kurta and her hair open with a tote bag, she looked so beautiful.I could not even blink my eye because I didn't want to miss even a second of seeing her." I said blushing and smiling

"Okay there buddy, I am gonna stop you right here, you have gone to college for just one day and already simp over a girl. Oh boy! Samay and

I are gonna have so much fun with seeing you puppy around her" Tej said making face that mocks me so much.

"Whatever, one day you would be witnessing the greatest love story ever, thats mine and hers for sure. Anyways lets meet early for college tomorrow we have to go and register for the upcoming fest for the freshers and maybe I see her" I say casually.

"Sure, now you will be like those lovers basically in your Shahrukh Khan era now. Lets register and then go for PS, I will call Samay and let him know about your little miss perfect also." saying this Tej left.

At night, post dinner I was just thinking about her again and again, she had a sharpness in her eyes, like someone who has seen a lot of troubles but then her face full of compassion and peace. Man, I know "she is the one". I wish tomorrow I get to see her again and I get to know her name. Will she talk to me? God, only girls I have ever talked to are either my sisters or my best friends sisters. I know going to all boys school is worst when you have to go talk to a girl you like.

Next day I woke up early and wore something casual yet comfortable. And I went to pick up Tej and Samay.

As soon as Samay entered he started with "Thank us Kanan, we are giving you training to pick and drop her in future." Tej and Samay started laughing and I made my usual okay okay face.

Inner me was agreeing and blushing but yeah whatever.

We went inside the college and asked the student council about the registration for the fest for freshers. He said "You guys just made it on time, today was the last day. On the right side classroom, ask for Cheryl , she is the fresher who is looking into the registration."

We went into the classroom and looked for Cheryl. She was dressed elegantly but nothing could beat her.

CHERYL

"Hi, I am Tej, we are here for registering for fest for freshers." Tej talked with Cheryl.

While my eyes were searching for her, where was she? I want to see her.

"Hello, do you guys want booth also? or just registration for the fest for freshers?" Cheryl asked all three of us.

"Just registration would be good. I am Samay and he is Kanan." Samay pointed towards me and I gave me a warm smile, too which Cheryl smiled back.

"Here you go guys, the fest for freshers is tomorrow. The booths are from 3pm - 7pm, post that there are some dance performances followed by dinner and DJ night. Looks like Kanan is looking for someone, maybe I can help?" Cheryl asked me in a fun way but with an intention to help.

I was about to reply when Tej jumped in and said " Our boy is in his lover era." All three of them i.e. Tej, Samay and Cheryl had a good laugh while I was getting uncomfortable.

"Sounds like we are here for a great love story." Cheryl commented.

"Yeah, just he doesn't knows her name or basically any thing about her." Samay added.

These guys need to stop giving the details and embarrassing me. I was already making weird faces.

"Seems like you need help buddy, good for you, that you know me now because of the registration I know everyone. If you see her tell me and I will help you." Cheryl said and I smiled like a lovesick puppy.

"Thats good. Thank you Cheryl." I said, thats first thing I have said in last 10 minutes conversation.

Then Tej, Samay and I went to canteen after biding goodbye to Cheryl. I really thought Cheryl would be in not to talk category but she is sweet just looks rough and non approachable.

Well atleast now I can get to know her , I really hope I meet her at the Fest for Freshers.

Chapter 3

Letting Go

Avantika's pov :

Its been days since Moksh and I broke up. Honestly un-loving a person is much more difficult than actually being in love. Its all easy and nice with the right one. With Moksh it was never as easy but yes he was nice, atleast I would like to believe it.

It was first day of college, I was clear about staying away from guys because they are all douche bags and nothing good can happen until you start to date a guy who is ready to be a man for you.

I wore a simple outfit , nothing fancy to gain attention. I always knew college would be the place I will be the best version, but right now nothing feels more inviting than crying in a corner and then ordering a cup of ice-cream.

Life is full of tragedies and my life full of drama with all fucking things happening at one time.

Mom and dad are discussing about business, so it's safe to say my marriage is also business deal for them. I never dreamt of marrying Moksh because I know my parents won't ever support it because of the cultural difference, but sure I have no hopes of getting a guy who would love me. Business deal marriage sounds good to me.

I left home for college, and went to my classroom. I scanned the room in a glance and I found a girl who looked like she won't talk and pretty unapproachable. Man, I don't know these kind of people are my type. They would their business and I would mind mine. After Moksh's trauma, I want to go out and explore and not get myself babysitting another person.

I sat next to her, and as soon as I sat she started talking, why god why? Right seriously? I hope she is nice.

"You can seat somewhere else also?" She said.

"Hi, I am Avantika, I know I can, but you seem like you could use some company." I said with a smile.

"Hey, I am Cheryl, sure I would love a company." She said smiling back.

There was something about her, she felt distant but homely also. College atleast gave me a friend.

"Avanti, you okay? You look like you are about to water the whole of Rajasthan with your eyes." Cheryl said while patting my back.

"Its not like that, I am okay. I just had a breakup few days back." I said trying to hold back the memories.

"Aww sweetie, how are you holding up? Do you want to talk about it? Lets get out and talk about it. " Cheryl asked with concern.

"That would be nice, thank you so much for doing this. I haven't really talked about the breakup to anyone." I said

We went to canteen and I told her everything about Moksh and my relationship. There was no detail I left except for the incident. I am not yet ready to talk about it. It was one if my most terrific horrors.

"Avanti, baby you will find someone who loves you more than that douche bag. He is a piece of shit, why would you date a guy like him? Good thing is you and I are friends, I will approve your guys now and you get to choose from the approved ones only. Lets be happy you got off from a bad relationship. I know it's hard but trust me its the best thing that happened to you. " Cheryl said and it really made me comfortable. She is my first friend in college and she is has been nothing but a sweetheart to me.

"You are really sweet, I am happy I found you in college." I said smiling through my puffy eyes.

We were just eating in canteen when Cheryl pointed towards the poster, fest for freshers.

" We should totally go. It will be fun and we even get to check out some guys." She said happily.

"Sounds like a good idea except for guys part. Lets register, they even have booths." I added as response.

We went to the student council, and luckily they needed volunteers in registering the freshers as the fest work load was a lot, Cheryl decided to volunteer the registration part, while I joined the booth duty.

"Your work Cheryl would be registering the freshers and giving them the details about the event, while Avantika you will assign booths and help if anyone wants to get information about booths." Student council member guided us.

"Yes, perfect." we both said in excitement.

We had to report from tomorrow, I bid my farewell for the day to Cheryl and came back home. I cooked dinner. I love cooking a lot, its my therapy.

It was easy to just be busy then think about Moksh and the relationship. I am going to take some time before I heal and get back. I know there are going to be the learnings.

Next day I woke up excited, it was a great deal since I didn't feel this feeling in months. I texted Cheryl to meet me at the college gate in an hour. I showered and ate my breakfast. I decided to wear a simple brown kurti and leave for college.

I met Cheryl and decided to go the class where registration was suppose to happen. Apparently today college was more crowded because of admission of the freshers. I went ahead with booth duty and Cheryl with her registration work. We would meet at canteen during lunch.

The day was going quite okay, I was even suppose to volunteer in admission work until lunch break. Then I decided to go to a cafe with Cheryl. We both talked and bonded and vibe, even though we both are exactly opposite personalities.

I reached home all tired, and slept right after dinner. Tomorrow, is the last day for the registration and but obviously most busy day because everyone registers on last day. Cheryl has lots of work tomorrow.

We decided to go college early and I picked Cheryl's coffee. We met and then got to work. She was so happy I got her coffee and thanked me. She told me to meet after the college hours.

Today was most busy and hectic day, I got so many people to register for booths.

One of the girls asked me if she would partially volunteer her booth, she was setting up a desert type booth. She likes to bake and deserts is her therapy. I told her to be relaxed, I will be there to help her out.

Later Cheryl and I went to cafe and talked about our day and gossiped a bit. Come on, girls gotta feed her mind also.

"You know, I met a guy named Kanan, apparently he likes a girl in college and he doesn't even know her name. He even has two other friends, Tej and Samay. They are nice guys,all innocent. I told Kanan I will help him find his girl tomorrow." Cheryl told me and I listened carefully

"Man, do guys even do this? pretty sure Kanan would like her for her body type and nothing else. Guys are never innocent Cheryl. And if Kanan actually likes this girl even before he knows her, he is insane or the girl is incredibly lucky. Anyways you did a great job offering to help Kanan. We are in for some love story." I say

"Whatever it is, this is going to be fun. And remember there are still good guys out there. I am going find you one whenever you are ready or the guy is hot." Cheryl said laughing.

"We will see that." I say plainly.

We left for home then. Tomorrow is fest for freshers, the event starts at 3 pm, we have to be there by 2 pm to set up booths and be the extra hands.

I was thinking about what Cheryl said, after my dinner before my sleep, do guys do seriously see a girl and be obsessed with her? I mean till when they are obsessed? Until they get a girl to themselves and then treat her like shit. God why I am thinking about this all, it's not like I am the girl. I am just upset with the whole breakup and in my hating man era.

Anyways, Avanti let's go to sleep, we have to get dressed tomorrow. I haven't decided an outfit yet. But that I will do tomorrow.

All and all I know whatever happened didn't happen in my favour right now but one day I will know why it happened. Moksh was not the wise decision but he did teach me certain things.

I sleep thinking these things.

____Thank you so much guys for reading

Let me know what you guys think about it! All the suggestions and story predictions are welcome.

Please vote, comment and share.

Lots of loveAvantika

Chapter 4

F irst Meet

Avantika's POV:

I woke up early the next morning. I went for a walk since I wanted to be fresh and just have a glow post walk. Today was an important day. I was feeling weird but in a good way. I came back home and had shower. I decided to wear a white kurti which was very elegant with jeans, paired with my favourite sneakers and jhumkas.

I left for college and picked up Cheryl from her house. She was looking amazing as always. She and I are exact opposite aesthetics. She was wearing a white formal pant with pink top. She was looking pretty.

We reached college and were assign to do all the last minutes changes and arrangements. Later the crew was asked for a lunch which was super fun.

After that we started to arrange booths, there were booths in almost all categories - games, deserts, snacks, books, photos, and all one can imagine. Cheryl went to do her pending work

I find the girl who asked for my help yesterday. She greeted me and asked me to get the freshly baked goodies from her car right outside and I started to do so. I carried cheesecakes, they looked so delicious. Then cookies, but I had to go meet the council head also. I decided to meet head first and then keep cookies as they were last batch to be carried and also the most important ones. I met the head and he asked me to join the committee and interview for the core members. I was overjoyed and I was happily walking towards the booths for which I had to walk through a long corridor.

Kanan's Pov:

I woke up late as I ended up thinking about meeting her today. She would so cute if she wore a white chikankari kurti and jeans. Boy, I really want to see her today.

I shower and decide what to wear, when I saw my shirt was pressed even my white t-shirt.

I went near Tej's house and Samay was there already. They both were late and I was already getting irritated, can't they understand I have to find her and try to talk to her. I decided to take my bike and lead the way. Tej and Samay were coming together on Tej's bike.

We reached the college and parked our bikes. We were about to enter the college when Tej's phone had a notification. He had joined BUMBLE (a dating app). Samay looked at Tej and gave his evil smile. Out of us three, Tej was the one who could get any girl he wanted. Samay wanted to be nosy and check out the notification. I decided to forward, I am least interest in the dating apps.

I started to walk down the corridor at the end of which the booths were arranged. While I was walking I saw her in a white Kurti. She was about to fall when I jumped in and she was in my arms, but the cookie jar in her hand falls down and breaks. My heartbeat was so fast, I wish she doesn't hear it. Her eyes were closed because ofc she though she would fall.

She looks so fucking beautiful, how can someone be so beautiful. I was red and I was blushing hard, but I was trying to control my emotions.

(The fall imagine, Avantika being in Kanan's arms, the expressions and posture are same as the picture above)

She opened her eyes and widened her eyes in shock, disbelieve and bit of anger.

She straightened herself and adjusted her dress, while I was staring at her, I didn't even realise until she started talking.

"hello, i...i...sorry...i mean thank you for saving me .....but cookies." she was confused about what to say.

"What umm?" I smiled in apology as I didn't understand a word.

"You could have saved the cookies instead, it were for the booth." She said.

Is she for real? She was ready to get hurt and fall, just because the cookies were for booth!!!

"I am sorry, I didn't see the cookie jar. I was walking when I saw you slipping. I decided to stop you from falling. Did you get hurt?" I said in a concerned tone.

I usually don't talk, but with her I am able to. She surely has something about her.

"I am sorry it's just I promised a girl I would help her set up booth, she asked to get her cookie jar but I had to meet the head of council. So I got some great news, I was happy and I guess that's why I slipped. Thank you so much for saving me. But the cookies?" She said looking at me, she is so helpful. I was simply smiling.

" Don't worry, I would never let you fall. About cookies, we can get it from a bakery near by." I suggested.

"Umm, I am not sure, How will be get there so fast?" She said worriedly.

"Come, I will show you." saying this I lead the way and she followed.

"By the way, what's your name?" She asked curiously.

"I am Kanan, Kanan Singhania." I said while walking.

I could sense her getting relaxed and happy. I didn't understand why though.

We went to the area where my bike was parked. Thankfully, Tej and Samay had left. I don't them to see me with her. I want to know her. She looks like a beautiful mystery.

Thank you so much guys for reading.

I am sorry to update late.

Also next chapter , do you guys want Avantik's pov about this incident or continuation.

Let me know.

I am so grateful for all the people reading my story.

Thank you so much.

Lots of love,

Avantika.

Chapter 5

W as it a date?

Avantika's POV:

I was walking and suddenly my leg slipped, god why do I keep embarrassing myself. I closed my eyes so that I don't see myself falling, but I felt a firm grip around my waist. I didn't have courage to open my eyes for a minute but the grip was quite strong and I could eyes on me.

I opened my eyes to see a guy holding me. It was like a scene straight out of movie.

The guy was handsome, he looked like a gentleman but he was blushing hard. Do guys even are like him anymore?

His stripped shirt was fitting him perfectly. I was thinking all this while in his arms, and I didn't want to stand up yet. But I realised I had to. I adjusted my dress and started talking aka blabbering.

"hello, i...i...sorry...i mean thank you for saving me .....but cookies." I said in a confusing voice.

"What umm?" He replied in very polite voice.

God he is making me nervous. I try to speak again.

"You could have saved the cookies instead, it were for the booth." I said in a plain voice.

"I am sorry, I didn't see the cookie jar. I was walking when I saw you slipping. I decided to stop you from falling. Did you get hurt?" He said in a concerned tone, after thinking for few seconds that felt like a minute.

"I am sorry it's just I promised a girl I would help her set up booth, she asked to get her cookie jar but I had to meet the head of council. So I got some great news, I was happy and I guess that's why I slipped. Thank you so much for saving me. But the cookies?" I said while I was smiling to not make it obvious that I was blushing somewhere and nervous. I don't want to fuck it up.

" Don't worry, I would never let you fall. About cookies, we can get it from a bakery near by." He suggested. God, he is sweet, he wants to help me. AWWW CUTU.

"Umm, I am not sure, How will be get there so fast?" I said worriedly.

"Come, I will show you." saying this he lead the way and I followed like a little puppy.

"By the way, what's your name?" I asked curiously, so that I can stalk him up and uk know him.

"I am Kanan, Kanan Singhania." He said while walking in front of me.

I was happy and relaxed. I have had heard about him and I wanted to meet him , but meeting him in this way is way to crazy. He is sweet, not creepy as of now.

I saw him coming to the parking area, he felt relaxed knowing there is no one around.

"This is my bike. We will go and get cookies and be back in no time. " He said in very friendly manner.

"There is no way I am sitting on a bike with you. What if you don't ride properly?" I said in shock and disbelief.

Last time I sat on a bike was with Moksh and it was just after I told him about it. He pushed me to the ground. My heart beated so fast in panic and I didn't know if I wanted to or not but I would love to know an option. I was thinking when Kanan's voice interrupted my thoughts.

"Don't worry, Cookie. We are going to go safely and come back safely. Maybe if you want we can even try their cheesecakes. They make the best cheesecakes." He said calmly. I think he sensed I was getting nervous. His voice had some sort of calming effect on me.

"I love cheesecakes. Promise me you will drive carefully!." I said while making a cute puppy face.

"Thats perfect, lets have cheesecake, get some cookies and I promise to drive safely, Cookie" He said and I smiled like my old self.

I said on his bike and my arms folded. He started the bike and was driving carefully.

He turned back to ask me, if I was comfortable and I replied with yes.

Soon we reached the bakery and i got down. He parked the bike and we went inside. It was very pretty. We walked inside.

"You sit, I will order cookies for take away and a cheesecake for you, Coo kie."He said and went for giving order.

The interiors of the cafe were so pretty. I saw Kanan ordering a cheesecake, I wish he gets strawberry cheesecake, I love strawberry cheesecakes a lot.

A while later, Kanan came holding a plate of cheesecake. My eyes sparkled like a kid.

" I really wanted you to get strawberry cheesecake. I love them. Thank you!!" I said and dig in to get the first bite.

"It's so delicious. Have a bite , here." I took a spoonful and fed him cheesecake myself.

"It's so good!" He was clearing blushing.

"So, Kanan how much do I have to pay you?" I asked while stuffing my mouth with this amazing cheesecake.

"You don't have to pay me, Cookie." He said smiling.

"That's not how it works, lets split or else I will never come and have cheesecakes with you again." I said in rather dominating voice. I want to come and have cheesecakes with him. It's so much fun

"Okay, okay. You have to pay me this much amount." He showed me the calculator in his mobile.

I paid him, while our order was ready.

He and I talked about normal stuffs. He asked me about my Instagram handle and we exchanged phone numbers.

He dropped me to the college gate and then we walked inside together.

"By the way, I heard you like a girl in college. I bet she is very lucky. Whats her name?" I asked out of curiosity.

As soon as he was about to answer, someone called me.

"Avantika, we need your help." The member of student council called me.

"I am so sorry, I have to leave. We will talk about it post booth duty. Let me take you for coffee. You have helped me so much. 7:30 pm, meet me at the college gate." I said and left in hurry.

I saw him smiling while I left. Was it a date? I wonder to myself. He is a sweetheart.

"Hey, please let's not tell this to anyone yet. I mean you helping me." I texted him.

"Don't worry cookie, you can be assured. Work carefully. Don't fall." He texted me back immediately.

I liked the message and began to work.

Thank you so much guys for reading.

I am so grateful for you all.

Please vote, comment, share

Let me know how you feel about this chapter.

Lots of love,

Avantika

Chapter 6

Getting to know

Kanan's POV:

Did it just happen? I went out with Avantika? She sat on my bike and we had cheesecake together? She fed me.

Kanan stop, you yourself saw she is way too kind and she goes out of her way. Didn't you realise just for some cookies , she was okay to get hurt.

It's true no one can understand women.

Anyway I head down to the booths and finally find Tej and Samay. Tej was looking at girls as usual and Samay was seeing what he wants to eat.

I went upto my boys and started talking," Haha, Tej keep stalking girls. Someone will surely come and slap you, Samay and I would pretend we don't know."

"Okay Mr. India, where were you for the last 1.5 hours? And about girls, they are so hot. Even you can stare." Tej said while still looking for a girl.

"I had some urgent work of dad, so I had leave. Okay bro." I said plainly.

"I want to have some snacks. Lets look around."

The fest was amazing and I was looking around to see. Samay saw a small vada pav booth and jumped to the booth. He ordered 3 vada pav with spicy chutney.

"Bro, this is so awesome." Samay said while taking another bite of this wholesome vada pav.

"I haven't tasted something so delicious, I really like this so much." Tej added to Samay.

"I know, we should go on exploring best places to eat in Mumbai. Or maybe we can start a youtube channel." I added while having a food orgasm.

"We can do it." They both agreed to me.

We completed the vada pav and started to stroll. We spotted a photo booth. We decided to take some weird photos.

The photo booth is well decorated and I wish Avantika And I could take photos here. Someday we will be able to take photos in public.

Our photos came weird but good. I will frame and hang in my room.

Then Samay suggested we go to dessert booths because he needs cookies.

I was overjoyed, thats an understatement. Maybe she is there.

"Can we have 1 chocochip cookie, 1 cinnamon cookie and 1 blueberry compote cookie. Please." Samay said to the girl in the booth.

"Sure, just a sec." The girl replied while indicating to the prices on the board.

Samay pointed towards me and asked me to pay. More than my non existent girlfriend, these guys make me pay.

"Avantika, can you please take out one of each chocochip, cinnamon and blueberry compote cookies for the guy there." The girl said to another girl who was handling payments.

There she was, she took out cookies and placed them on a plate and gave it to me with a bright smile. I smiled back and gave the cookies to Samay , my hungry princess.

Then I turned back to see her indicating me towards her watch. It was almost 6:45 pm.

We had to leave around 7 pm.

I gave her a thumps up. She saw it.

"Guys, I have to leave for some work. I will meet you guys tomorrow, lets go for a movie tomorrow afternoon." I said while they were eating cookies.

"Again? Okay let's go for a movie tomorrow. If you bail I am going to kill you Kanan Singhania." Tej told me in an angry way.

"I won't, bye guys." I said and I left for the main gate.

Avantika's pov :

"Hey, I have to leave for some work. It was super fun to work with you." I said to the girl whose booth I was handling.

"Hey, sure. Thank you so much for helping me." Aadhavi said. (girl who had dessert booth)

"Your welcome dear." said and left to find Cheryl.

"Ma'am, I will be bid you bye since I have to leave for some urgent work." I said to Cheryl in a fun way.

"What? Why? No you are not leaving right now. The party is about to start and I want you to meet guys and have fun." Cheryl said in a way which is dominating.

"I don't wish to meet any guy and I am telling you that don't find me a guy. I don't like parties. I am leaving, see you tomorrow." I said in a polite tone.

"Okay, as you say then. Let's go for movie tomorrow afternoon." Cheryl said in bit convincing way.

"Sure. Bye, have fun." I said and started to walk away when suddenly my phone beeped.

I saw a notification from Kanan.

KS : Let's meet at the small tea shop near college, so no one sees us.

Avantika : Coming in 5 mins.

I replied and started walking. Soon I reached the tea shop. And I saw him sitting on his bike and waiting for me.

I reached there and said him hi, he said hi back.

"So, Miss Avantika what do you want to do?" He asked curiously.

"Do you like tea or coffee?" I asked him

"Tea" He replied immediately

Thats perfect. I ordered two tea parcel and got two paper cups.

"Let's go" I then came near his bike and asked him to drive as I give instructions.

I made him drive to carter road. It is a place I wanted to visit since a long time.

It is so beautiful and one can only think of the beauty of it.

I asked him to park and follow me. He did follow without asking any questions.

And finally we saw the perfect spot.

"It is truly amazing Cookie." Kanan said while looking at me.

They sun had just set. There is still some light in the sky. We sat on the rocks and I poured our hot chai (tea) in the paper cups.

It was so peaceful.

"You know, I always wanted to come here. The waves, clouds, rocks, there is something about this place that is so mesmerising. There is so much peace even though it is so chaotic. I like how it makes you feel." I said while looking at him and having a plain smile on my face.

"Thats true. Its peaceful and its the kind of chaotic mind likes." Kanan added while sipping on his tea.

"So kanan, tell me about yourself but don't include your name, school, education, religion, native in it." I said to Kanan who was confused at my way of asking.

After a pause, he smiled and answered.

"I never talked to a girl before you. I like romantic cliches. I make the best pastas according to my best friends. I believe we all have purpose in life and to be a good human is not only a necessity but also important. And I like your company." Kanan said and I smiled.

"That was a good introduction Mr Kanan Singhania. Did you never really talked to a girl? And when are you making pasta for me? I love pastas.

About being a good human I totally agree with you. Sometimes a small act of kindness goes a long way." I replied and he listened carefully.

"Only girls I have talked to are either sisters or my bestfriends' sisters. When do you want to eat pasta, cookie?" He said while I was looking at the sky and he was looking at me with a smile.

"Whenever you make them." I said

"Now, tell me about yourself." He is curious, hehe

"I had certain situations in my life, I regret . Loss is something which is inevitable but to forget that loss is more inevitable. I am really lucky in some ways to have people around me. I like to write and read." I sighed. It is hard but it feels good to say things like this.

"Thats quite deep. Whatever you went through, you are really strong to go through. You are lucky for people as well. I would love to read what you write." He said while finishing his tea.

"Someday, I will show you what I write. Do you want to have dinner?" I asked him.

"Sure but where?" He requestioned me.

"Well I will take you to my favourite pasta place, it's a street food joint." I told him and he instantly got happy.

"Sure, so does that mean I will have to drive?" He said in a funny way

"Yes, I am a passenger princess" I said in same tone as his.

"Ofc Princess." and he laughed.

We drove to the pasta place, it was 20 minutes away. I was happy and I felt safe. He is going to be a great friend. I know I know I don't trust guys, but he is really sweet.

We reached the place and I went ahead and ordered, while he parked the bike.

We sat on stools and soon our white sauce pasta arrived with two chocolate milkshake.

"Here, take the first bite and tell me how it is." I asked Kanan

He took the bite and he had a burst of flavours I feel.

"It's awesome. Cheesy, creamy, veggies." Kanan described.

"I know right" I started eating too.

We completed the pasta and chocolate milkshake, while general talks like my favourite movie and stuffs.

"Well I guess, I will leave now. It's getting late. My parents would worry about me." I told kanan.

"I will drop you, come sit." He offered.

"No, no I will take a train, don't worry." I said reassuring him.

"Let's take a picture for memory." He suggested

And then we took 4-5 photos and he dropped me till the station and didn't leave until my train moved out of his sight. Thats so much of a gentleman gesture. Today was so much fun but tiring day.

I just want to go home and sleep and thats exactly what I did after texting Kanan.

Avantika : I reached home, safely. Thank you so much for today. It was so much fun. Thank you for not telling anyone that we hanged out.

He replied almost immediately

KS: Hey, the pleasure is all mine. Even I had a great time myself, Cookie. Thank you and all is formality don't bother yourself so much. I won't tell anyone until you want me too.

Avantika: Thats nice. Tomorrow Cheryl and I going for a movie in afternoon.

KS: Tej, Samay and I are also going to movie tomorrow afternoon. Where are you going?

Avantika: Metro Inox

KS: Same, let's meet tomorrow then. Good night Avantika

Avantika: Good Night.

I was so tired that I slept almost immediately without having any other thoughts.

Next morning I woke up a bit late because of the tiredness. I saw I had a notification from an unknown number.

Unknown Number: I know, what I did was wrong Avantika. I regret it. But it was not my mistake only that happened, even you were involved. Stop telling people or else I will tell everyone what happened on 2nd November last year. If you don't want it to be public then just keep your mouth shut. Or else you know what can I do and what not

I was sweating a lot. No one can ever know what happened on 2nd November. I can't breathe.

Thank you so much guys for reading. I am so sorry for late update, I was unwell since last week. Thank you so much for understanding. I made this chapter long as a compensation.

I am so grateful for you all.

Please vote, comment, share

Let me know how you feel about this chapter. What you think about Kanan and Avantika.

Lots of love,

Avantika

Chapter 7

U nexpected News

Avantika's Pov:

I need to get hold of my breath. God why? Just when you gave me a good day you decided to bring my past back why? It's something no woman can ever forget even not in her widest dreams.

I decided to ignore it and take a shower, until there was another notification from the same number.

Unknown Number: Avantika, you know right I am not kidding about it. I need to know why did I get a message of a document from the hospital? What are you trying to do? Prove yourself innocent, you are good with your games but don't play them with me.

A message from hospital? After 8 months why? Should I go and check? But if he sees me there I will have no other option.I need to meet him, but I don't want to meet him. Last time we met was before 1 month of our break up. We had gone to hospital together. It was shady so he had to accompany me, because if something happens to me, my father would hunt him down.

Avantika : Can we meet? 11:30 am our old spot.

Unknown number: If you do anything that is over smart, I myself will tell everyone about what has happened. I think your dad will like it. Meeting you by 11:30 am.

I dressed up in a simple white kurta and plazo pants, and left after having breakfast.

I drove to the spot where I saw him after 10 months. I don't have a good feeling about it. I know I can never forgive him for what he did, even if it was unintentional I lost my piece of heart because of him. I loved him a lot since day one, but now because of the loss I had, sorry we had it is difficult to even hate him.

I park my scooty and enter the cafe. He was seating at our spot. God, this is so painful.

He still has the hat, I made for him. What is he trying to prove?

I move walk past and sit on the couch in the opposite direction. I cough to get his attention.

"Look who it is, Avantika Shah. How is the princess?" He said in a manner that was making me uncomfortable.

"What do you want Moksh? What has happened?" I asked because inside of me I am crying, tensed and also want to kill him.

"Darling, what is the hurry?" He said while touching my hands

"Stay away Moksh, tell me what is it, or else I will leave." I said in almost shaky voice.

"You can leave but then your father will get an email about your documents from the hospital and then we all know what will happen. So why don't you sit and let me do the talking, sweetheart." He said in an authoritative voice.

"Hello ma'am and sir, it's lovely to see you after long time. The regular order? A hazelnut latte and one cold coffee?" We were interrupted by our old waiter. Moksh and I used to come here a lot during the time we were dating. He would always order a cold coffee and I loved my hazelnut latte.

"Sure." Moksh told the waiter.

"So where were we? Ah yes, a got a notification from the hospital regarding your reports. Why didn't you take care of it? I accompanied you to the hospital wasn't it enough? Avantika I don't have time and I have no interest in you, please make that clear. Whatever we had is over. I am forwarding the message to you and please make sure I am never bothered about it ever again." He said all in a very straight forward voice.

"I had no choice but to give your number, since my number was monitored back then. I know you have no interest, because of you we had to visit a hospital. You don't need to be worried. I will handle everything from now on. You could have told me this on message also?" I told him with a calm voice.

"Whatever happened, happened. Take care of yourself. No one will ever know what happened, I promise. I didn't want to message because you would not have taken seriously otherwise." Saying this he left all over again.

I sat there processing what happened, I asked for cheque from waiter. He told me sir had already paid. I need to go to hospital immediately. Why after 8 months hospital wants me to be there?

I drove to the hospital, it was 40 minutes away from the cafe. I was lost. What happened with Moksh, I didn't understand. Deep down I know he cares for me, maybe he doesn't. I know there are some questions which will be unanswered but this one "Did he never really loved the news even for a second?"

I reached the hospital and visited the doctor who had asked for me, her name was Ms. Kanak Gupta.

"Hello doctor, I am Avantika Shah. I got a message you want to see me. Is everything okay?" I asked her with deep concern in my voice.

"Avantika, come. I needed to speak with you in private, so I asked hospital to send you a message. I just need to check once and then I will let you know everything." She said in very calming tone.

I just smiled back at her not knowing what to expect. I am clearly worried. She took me to the observation and checked me. She asked me to be relaxed and some questions related to the past. I was getting uncomfortable but I answered them all.

"Avantika, I am sorry but I need to tell you something. I need you to be relaxed and hear me. You need to hold yourself strong." Doc said in very concerning tone.

She told me everything and I could not control my tears, it was one of my biggest fears. This can't happen. No, No, NO, NO.

"Avantika, please breathe. I know it is heavy news, but there are options. You don't want to tell anyone about it?" She was getting worried for me.

"NO, I am fine. I don't want to talk to anyone." I said her in a plain voice while sobbing.

"That is all I wanted to tell you. Please feel free to talk to me about anything you want to know." She said while patting my back.

"Thank you doctor, just a favour i need." I asked her while she was calming me.

"Yes dear, tell me" she said with a warm smile.

"Please change the number on the hospital register. The number there is not reachable for good." I handed her a small piece of paper which had my number.

I left and went in my car. I don't know what to do. This can't happen god. After everything, you don't get to take this god. I needed this, you knew I did.

I somehow manage my tears and then normal my voice. I picked up my phone to see messages from Cheryl.

Cheryl: Meeting you in 15 minutes at Metro Inox. Don't you dare cancel Avantika. I love you.

I need to meet her. I guess it's better to take off my mind. But I don't feel like anything. ____

Thank you so much guys for reading. I am so grateful for you all.

I know, last chapter was extremely happy and this quite opposite, that is how life is sometimes. Unexpected and unpredictable. I will try to upload as much as I can.

Please vote, comment, share

Let me know how you feel about this chapter.

Lots of love,

Avantika

Chapter 8

Movie Time

Avantika's Pov:

If I go in this dress then Cheryl will be angry. We are going to watch Barbie, and the rule to watch it is wearing pink. It's going to be a girls' date. I drive to a nearby mall and see some clothes. I go in zara and check some options.

I finally liked a fit on me, it is not my usual but it helped me distract myself from the news.

I was looking sexy and cute at the same time. I paid for the dress and drove to the cinema hall. I call Cheryl and ask her where is she, as usual Cheryl madam was late.

After 10 minutes Cheryl walked in with a pretty pink outfit. It was so obvious we are going for barbie.

I saw kanan, he was looking handsome. He was with Tej and Samay. Cheryl goes upto the boys and say hi.

Kanan Singhania

Samay

Tej

"Hi" Kanan, Tej and Samay replied with warmth to Cheryl.

"Why are you guys here? Are you following us Tej? Anyways this is Avantika." She announced.

"Yes, except from following you I have no other work sweetheart. You are so beautiful I can't stay away." Tej started irritating Cheryl

"Guys, calm down. We don't need a war right now. Anyways we are here for different movies. Lets enjoy and grab dinner together?"I interrupted before Cheryl would day anything.

"Hi, I am kanan, dinner sounds good." Kanan shook my hands and we all went for our movies.

Kanan, Tej and Samay were here for Oppenheimer and we were here for barbie.

"Tej seems to like you. He is your type also." I teased Cheryl.

"Maybe, Maybe not. Who knows." She said casually.

"If he would come to watch barbie with you, you would have loved it won't you?" I asked because she seems interested but would deny.

"I don't know. We are finding a guy for you, not me baby. Just relax and enjoy." She said avoiding the conversation.

Kanan's pov:

I took my phone, while Tej and Samay were buying popcorn and pepsi because our hungry princess needs food. I texted Avantika.

Kanan: You look really beautiful, Cookie.

She texted within 2 minutes.

Cookie: You don't look bad yourself, Kanan.

I smiled but then these idiots interrupted me. We went inside and watched the movie. It was a good 7/10 movie. I really feel like the movie was bit long.

We left the movie hall and waited in the waiting area in the mall. Soon our barbies arrived and they seemed happy.

"How was the movie guys?" Avantika asked all three of us.

"Our movie was amazing. It was somewhere about female friendship." Cheryl said in excitement.

Cheryl and Avantika are looking happy post movie.

"Our movie was okayish." Tej said while looking at Cheryl.

"I want some golgappe." Avantika said in her cute baby voice.

"Kanan loves golgappe. He eats 3-5 plates at once." Tej said again he is staring at Cheryl.

"So let's make Avantika and Kanan have a golgappe competition." Cheryl said in fun way.

"What does the winner gets?" Avantika asked in enthusiasm.

She gets excited like a little child. I like her this side. Although she looks little tense. I should give her a good prize if she wins.

"Winner gets a cheesecake." I said to all of them.

Avantika looked at me and smiled, felt like she was saying thank you.

"Let's go this small stall near mall." Cheryl suggested.

Then we all went to the cars and Tej, Samay and I were in my car. Cheryl and Avantika were in Avantika's car. She took the lead since Cheryl knew the place. I followed and soon we reached the destination.

"Let's keep a condition, who ever stops first has to buy the winner a cheesecake." Samay said.

"Let's do it Mr. Kanan Singhania." Avantika said in a funny way.

We started eating one after one. Soon Cheryl started cheering and Tej started to cheer me because he wanted to compete with Cheryl.

We had 4 plates and I was full, I gave up.

"I won." Avantika screamed.

She was so happy.

"Let's buy you cheesecake, my lady." I said to Avantika who was almost done with golgappe for atleast 1 week.

"I am getting late, Can you drive me home Tej?" Cheryl asked.

"Sure, Kanan can I take your car?" Tej asked me.

"Ha sure, drive safely." I gave the car keys.

"Tej, I am going to join you. I have to go out tomorrow morning." Samay said to Tej.

"Bye guys, today was so much fun we should go out more, all of us." Cheryl suggested.

"Sure, sunday morning Marines?" Avantika asked.

"Done. Bye. Good Night." Cheryl, Tej and Samay said and eventually.

Everyone left, now it was just me and cookie.

"Do you want to drive or be passenger princess? I ask cookie.

"Passenger Princess." She said while looking away.

We drove to the cheesecake place we went yesterday. I got down and opened a door for her.

We went inside and I ordered her a strawberry cheesecake. She was happy, but she seemed tensed.

"Are you okay cookie?" I ask her in a concerned way.

"I am okay, just had a rough day." She said but there was a bit of sadness in her voice.

"Let's go for a walk? And we can talk about it if you want it?" I suggested and she said yes.

"I don't want to talk about it, but lets get ice cream."She said as she took the last bite of cheesecake.

She is clearly stressed or she has her periods around.

We ate ice cream and walked around the streets of Mumbai. I know I feel calm around her. She makes me feel calm and comfortable.

We were silent during our whole walk, it was peaceful and amazing. Soon it was late.

"I will drop you home and then go home." Cookie said to me while we reached the car.

She drove the car and I sat next to her. We reached my home and I said her good night, take care, drive safely and message me once she reaches home.

Thank you so much guys for reading. I am so grateful for you all.

Please vote, comment, share

Let me know how you feel about this chapter.

Lots of love,

Avantika

Chapter 9

P ooja

Avantika's Pov:I reached home pretty late, so it was obvious my parents would be on their way to blame me for all the things I haven't done in my life.

"I don't even know you any more Avanti, what have you turned into? What time is it? Do girls of a good household come home so late? What are you wearing?Again all this? I don't know how much more shame you will bring to this family. Your dad is a very reputed businessman, he built this empire on his own, unlike you. What do you do all day? Go back to your room and tomorrow we have Pooja, be ready at 7 am. We have guests coming over. I want you to be in a saree. Your dad's business partner,Mr Chirag Rawat would be there. He has a son. Be like a good daughter." My mom just busted the information on me.

"Why is Chirag uncle coming? And why do I have to know about his son?" I ask mom, who is gonna give me another reason of how ungrateful and shameful my daughter is.

"Chirag uncle is probably going to be your father in law. Please behave and go back to your room." She yelled at me and so I left the hall and went to my room.

If the news wasn't enough, I have a to deal with the fact my parents have fixed my marriage also? In my life do I have any choice of my own? God, just give me strength.

I quickly change the clothes and take my phone. I had to text Kanan. He has been so sweet today. He tried to ask me what had happened. I couldn't tell him or anyone else. I want to keep it to me. I already have enough issues at my own to tell someone and have risk of being exposed.

Some truths we can't live with and some truths our loved ones can't live with. It's better to keep some truths as a hidden facts.

I take my phone and text Kanan.

Avantika: Hey, I reached home a while back. Today was amazing, thank you for letting me win and not forcing me to talk. It was really sweet of you.

He texted me within minutes.

KS: Hey, cookie don't bother yourself so much. I understand you have valid reason not to tell me.

I don't know what it is about him that's so irresistible. He understands the reason even when I am silent? Is this some kind of test God. I hope you know you are giving a broken heart hope here.

Avantika: Its late, let's sleep. Good night KS

KS: Good night cookie . Take care

I am unable to sleep. The visit to doctor keeps replaying in my head. It's 3 am in the morning. I get up from bed and slowly go to my study table and take my journal. I write about today, what happened and how I feel about it.

I sit there in silence, until I am asleep on study desk. I woke up to the sound of alarm, it's 5:30 in the morning.

The weather outside looks pleasant. The clouds look beautiful.

I take a shower and then select a blue saree with some silver jhumka and a necklace. I do a light make up and put a bindi.

I go down and see mom and dad dressed up in Indian attire.

I go to mom and ask her what I can help her with.

"Just stay away from any boy in the Pooja. Chirag uncle will be here any time. Just behave and stay away from trouble. You can sit in the Pooja." Mom said while instructing all the house servants.

I sit in Pooja quietly and pray to help myself get rid of the pain. To find a way my parents love me again. I hope I find a person who never makes me feel incomplete and never ever makes fun of all the love and care I have to offer. I sit in Pooja while the priest performs the ceremony.

I heard my parents welcoming someone. It must be Chirag uncle.I get up and go and touch his feet.

"Be happy my child. She has grown up so much. She looks like she is ready for marriage." Uncle said with a smile.

"Yes, you know brother, they say girls grow up fast. Come inside and take the blessings." Dad welcomed him and took him to the sacred fire.

I was then instructed to take care of the guest and feed them well post Pooja.

I did the things that were assigned to me.I take a photo and upload it to my WhatsApp status.

I love my look. I like Indian attire so much. It has so much richness and value. People think it's not modern but the modern is the thinking not just clothes.

I then take a shower and change into a comfortable fit. I had nowhere to go except for a walk. I take walks in the evening. I started it after I broke up with Moksh. It helps me calm my mind and also makes me feel good about certain things.I like seeing nature and the weather is also pleasant nowadays.

I take my phone after a quick nap. I had so many notifications, I opened and slowly read them.

Cheryl : Replied to status - you look awesome babe. Sending all the cute guys your photo.

Avantika: Haha, no you are not. Thank you so much.

I reply and then I see Kanan has also replied to my status. Wow he sees my status.

KS : You look gorgeous Cookie.

Avantika: Thank you

I then replied to the rest of the people who mostly included family members and some old friends who I had lost touch with.

It was a calm day but does Chirag uncle actually want me to be his daughter in law? I am not ready to get married. I want to build my career. I want to become financially independent and then meet a person who is in love with me as much as I am in love with him.

Well anyways I am excited for tomorrow. It's Sunday. We all are going to the marines and then I will take them all to my favourite breakfast spot.

I sleep in bits and pieces. I woke up at the ring of alarm and got dressed. Kanan would pick up all of us since we decided only to take one car out.

He would pick me first so I texted him where is he.______________ ___________________________________Thank you so much for reading.I am so grateful for you reading.I know this chapter isn't cute or romantic.I just wanted to give a background about Avantika's family.It's an Indian household, I don't mean to hurt anyone's sentiments.I am sorry if I have hurted anyone.Let me know what you feel.Next chapter is going to be really special □

Lots of love,Avantika

Chapter 10

Magical Marines □

Kanan's pov :

Cookie : When are you coming?

Kanan : I will be there near your house in 5 mins.

I text her and drive again. We were going to the marines today. I decided to pick Avantika first because I had a surprise for her.

I made some cupcakes for her. She was stressed day before yesterday. So I thought cupcakes would make Cookie.

I reach near her house and she is wearing a beautiful light salwar. She looks so beautiful in Indian wear, like a princess.

"You look pretty as usual passenger princess." I say and she smiles in response.

"You don't look Kanan" she said in her cute voice.

I was wearing a shirt and basic jeans.

She sits in the car and makes herself comfortable.

"Check the backseat please." I say to her and she is completely clueless and in confusion.

She finds a box of cupcakes and takes it forward to her seat.

"Why cupcakes? Are they for me?" She asks hoping a yes for answer.

"You looked upset the other day. So I thought of making you some chocolate cupcakes. They are for you cookie." She looks at me so adorably and thinks for a moment.I don't know why she gets lost in the thoughts so often.

"That is really the sweetest thing anyone has done for me. I am surprised you know to bake. Let me taste and tell you how they are. They look and smell heavenly." Saying this she stuffed her mouth with a bite.

"Oh my god, they are soooo delicious. Since when do you know to cook?" She asks me while eating again.She is like a little baby.

"I learnt cooking when I was around 10 years of age. Simran aunty taught me cooking. She cooks really amazing. Some day I will take you to eat her hands chole bhature." I say but seems like she is enjoying cupcakes more.

"That's good. For sure. Today I was thinking to take you all for South Indian breakfast or a Gujarati thali." She is eating so cutely. How can a human be so cute.

" I guess we would make it to having brunch. We would be at marines till 10:30-11." I say while almost reaching Tej's house. She also had finished eating and we had successfully cleaned the evidence.

Tej hoped in. We picked up Cheryl and Samay next. While we were about to reach Marines, we started teasing Tej and Cheryl. They surely have some chemistry.

We soon reached marines. I parked the car while Avantika decided to stay with me while I park so she can complete her cupcake. She is a baby deep down.

I got down and opened door for her, she said thank you. We were walking, we had to cross the road. This girl is careless when it comes to crossing roads. I hold her hand for the first time to make her cross road safely. She looked at me dumbfounded. She was clueless, but she felt safe. She didn't react in a bad way infact she was smiling. I love her smile. Her hands are super soft.

I leave her hand and we walked to our friends.

There were people dancing on songs, selling stuffs and randomly asking people questions.

We all were standing; Avantika and I were standing next to each other. Tej and Cheryl were close to one another and then there was samay.

A person approached us and asked me since Avantika and I have been dating. "Oh no, you are mistaken. We are friends." I say to the guy, while hoping it was true.

"I just thought you guys are dating since you guys were holding hands." He said and I didn't even realise when she and I were holding hands. Neither did she nor did I have any objection to hold hands.

We just smiled at the guy. Then all of us decided to walk around Marines to see what is happening. Samay was navigating in front. Tej and Cheryl were walking together. Cookie and I were walking little behind then others. We were walking holding hands. It was the best feeling ever.

When suddenly a small boy knocked on my back.

"Sir, please buy madam a rose. She would like it, please sir." The boy began to sell the roses.

Cookie looked at me and smiled.

"Give me 3 roses" Cookie said while I removed the cash to give the guy.

"Give it to me" I say to the little guy and he does exactly the same.

I go on one knee and give the flowers to Avantika. She blushes real hard.

Everyone around us started to cheer.

"Thank you so much. That was kind of a gesture Kanan?" She asks me. She is confused.

"Yes and no" I say as I see her getting excited at yes and kind of upset at no.

I am not able to read her expressions properly.

" I will tell you late, cookie." I say to her and she is kind of upset with me, I can see her expressions.

We continue to walk. And she tightens the grip around my hand.

"I want to ask you something Kanan." Cookie asks me in a serious tone, as we keep walking.

"Anything, ask me." I say her in a composed tone.

"Who was the girl you liked when you joined the college?" She asks me. It wasn't a question, it seems like it was a test for her and me.

She is worried about being an option.

"You remember the time you wore a brown kurti to college? It was you, Avantika. The admission day I saw you, I was taken a back by your beauty.

There was something about you that just my body shiver. I was wanting to know you." I say her and she is kind of sobbing.

"Kanan, this is so romantic. I am flattered. I don't know what to say. You liked me since day one?" She is blushing and happy at the same time.

"Yes cookie, how can I not be liking you? You are so beautiful inside and out. You care about your people more than anything." I say her while holding her hand.

"KANAN why didn't you tell me? Why did you let me not know this all?" She was smiling.

"I wanted you to know me first. I don't want to force myself on you. It had to be you being comfortable with me even to tell you I like you." I say with utmost care. She was looking at me like a love sick puppy.

"Kanan why are you so much of a gentleman? I always got home thinking why he is so nice? I am glad I asked you today." She says while stopping suddenly.

"What happened cookie? You okay?" I ask her. But then she hugged me.

My whole world stopped. She was hugging me. It felt warm and felt home instantly. She is shorter in me in height so I can see her forehead, I wanna kiss her forehead. She is so perfect.

"I never had someone describe me in this way. You are really very sweet." We are still hugging when she says this. I don't want to let go of her, neither does she.

"Cookie, I am here okay? Do you want to go out with me?" I ask her, it's the perfect moment.

"Kanan, I would love to but I can't trust my destiny with love again. I lost a lot when I was in love last time." She is looking in my eye, she is scared. I don't want her to be scared.

"Cookie, I won't force you. But give me a chance? A date. If you still feel same I promise to be a friend for you always." I say reassuring her.

"A date tomorrow" she says and hugs me again.

"I have a perfect date for you, I will pick you at 8 am." I say her and we start walking towards our friends who were dancing.

We danced a bit, took lots of photos. Drank chai and sat there and enjoyed the moment. I was excited about tomorrow.

"I am hungry, let's go and have something." Cheryl said.

"Do you guys want to go and have a thali?" Cookie asks.

"I am in." Samay jumped in at the mention of thali.

"Let's go and have thali. This is gonna be the best thali of your life." Cookie says. She is excited, she likes feeding people.

We drive to gujjubhai ni thali at Kemps corner.

We sat in this way, Cookie and me in one side. Tej and Cheryl were sitting opposite with samay.

We ordered 5 thalis. It was a vintage place but the food smelled amazing.

The thali was amazing, the food was soulful. We all overate for sure. We all were all food-drunk.

We decided to take a small walk to digest the food. It was fun and I was feeling good because Avantika was next to me.

I drove back to everyone. We dropped Samay first then Cheryl and lastly Tej.

Now it was just cookie and me.

I was driving while my passenger princess was happy.

"So Mr. Kanan where are you taking me for a date?" She asks me, she is a curious kiddo.

"It's a surprise, sweetheart. I hope you will like it." I tell her and she is getting impatient.

"Just tell me something please" she makes a puppy face. That's my weakness.

"Just wear a traditional dress with some good jhumka. You look awesome in it." I say and she gets shy.

"So a saree or salwar?" She asks me.

"SURPRISE ME WITH IT" I tell her and she gets happy.

"Tell me what should be there on the date compulsorily?" I ask her and she thinks carefully.

"I think just be yourself. Let me know the real you that's enough." She says and looks at me lovingly.

"I will be there with the real Kanan, princess." She smiles at me.

I dropped her home. She was not willing to go I can tell. I don't even want her to go but she has to.

"I will pick you tomorrow princess. Don't be late we have a long day tomorrow. Thank you so much for giving me a chance. You won't regret it." I say to her as a reassurance.

"I will be waiting for you Kanan." She says and leaves.

I drive to a cake shop to order a bento cake.

I finalize this cake, because I am grateful for her to give me a chance. She is really kind to give me the benefit of doubt.

Then I move to florist. I want to get her a bouquet and a small tiyara of flowers.

I make bouquet of white flowers because she brings lot of peace in my life. Her presence feels good, home.

And a tiyara for my princess. I just want tomorrow to be about her. I want to make her feel special, she is too special for me.

I drive to my house, I keep flowers and tiyara in the car. It's almost 7 pm.

Just 13 hours before I am on a date with my girl. Tomorrow is so precious.

I decided to wear a shirt because she seems to like me in shirts. I am gonna ask her about what colour is her outfit so we can twin.

I am all set and excited for tomorrow.

Thank you so much for reading my chapter.

This chapter is special because it is the start of my babies' love story.

I Love you all for reading my book.

I am so grateful for you reading it.

Let me know what you guys feel.

Tell me what you feel like should improve.

Lots of love, Avantika

Chapter 11

D^{ate}

Kanan's pov :

I ask cookie which colour she is going to wear, she said I can wear a shade thats light.

I decided to wear a pink shirt because it looks happening.

I wake up at 6 am the following morning, to be honest I couldn't sleep the last night in excitement. I am on date with Avantika Shah.

I go for a walk to calm my nerves down and then come back and have shower.

I got out and take my phone to text her.

Kanan : "Don't have breakfast. Will pick you up in 45 minutes."

Cookie : "Sure, will be there. Excited"

She texted back immediately. I know it's a long shot. She is definitely hiding something but I don't want to force her. She is delicate but a lioness.

I take out a pink shirt and blue jeans.

I had out to go to Avantika's. Someday I won't have to pick her up, because she would be living with me. Okay I need to get my horses together.

I drove to her house. And I saw her. She was looking beautiful as always. She wore a beautiful pink suit.

"Good morning, you look sweet in pink Kanan." She compliments me for the first time.

"Good morning sunshine, you look like an Indian princess. Thank you for the compliment. Check the backseat please." I say to her and she puts her hand on the back seat to check the backseat.

She found the flowers and the tiyara.

"Why this?" She asked me while she was obviously excited and happy.

"Flowers for you, it's just a good start to a date I assume and how are you a princess without a crown, so I thought to get you a tiyara." I explain her and she looks at me with lot of love.

"That's very thoughtful Kanan, thank you. I love it." She holds the flowers close to her and puts tiyara on her hair.

"Where are we going?" She asks me ofc, my curious sweetheart

"If you wanna guess? Where do we go before starting every good thing?" I give her something to search her head.

While she was thinking I drove to the place.

"A temple?" She says she is not sure though.

"You are smart!" We are almost here." I say and she giggles.

We drove to the siddhivinayak mandir. It is a Ganesh mandir and quite famous in Mumbai. Last time I came here with Maa. It was 9 years ago, after her I never had the strength to go anywhere. She was the ray of my sunshine.

"I always wanted to go to a temple as a date. It's exciting." She clears and we get down.

The temple was super beautiful from outside. We then went inside and took some offering for God.

We went inside, there was some line but we finally made it to the god.

We handled the offerings to a priest and prayed.

"May you both be together always." The priest said and blessed us.

"Thank you." Avantika said.

We left the mandir and came back to the car.

"So, does that mean a yes?" I ask Avantika.

"What?" She was confused.

"The priest just blessed us for being together and you said thank you?" I ask and start to drive.

"Well don't get ahead of yourself. Where are we going next? I am hungry." She said in a cute way.

"Taking you to have breakfast only, princess." I say and she smiles.

We played some songs on our way to the restaurant. I know she likes South Indian breakfast.

"I love this place! How do you even know?" She asks me as I drove the car to a parking spot near her favourite restaurant.

"Sneak peek at your Instagram!!" I say and I get down and open door for princess.

I know she is hungry, she won't say but it's obvious.

We go in and order some masala dosa and filter coffee.

"Okay, let's dig in!" She said and took the first bite.

"This is so delicious!" She then made the second bite and fed me.

I like when she feeds me! Ofc it's a feeling I miss. Mom used to do that whenever I was not feeling well or we shared a good conversation. I miss her.

We ate calmly and talked a bit in the restaurant. Then we headed out in the car.

"Now where do we go?" She asks me.

"For that you need to solve this puzzle. I know you like spending time along with me. I am something you always wanted to do but never did romantically." She looks at me with some shock but then she thinks.

"Are we going to Bandstand?" She guessed it.

"Yes, but in evening. Right now we are going for some street shopping and then we will go to an art gallery. Cheryl once told me you write. So I thought art gallery would be perfect for you." I say and her eyes are sparkling with happiness.

"Thats perfect, Jaan." She said and I blushed I mean why not.

I drove to Colaba, it was a short drive and I stopped at a small book vendor. I always thought she is nerd and well she loves books.

She got down and told me to sit in car since its traffic there. I waited for like 15-20 minutes until I started to see her again.

She had few books in her hand and small pouches of something, I can't see though. She is so happy, her smile is something I could die for any day. She is my sunshine.

"What did you get, princess?" I ask her as soon as she got in car. Around her I get excited about small things also.

"A couple of books and anklets. You know, I love anklets. I like the sound it produces." She says as we drive towards art gallery.

"What did you get me?I ask her, I didn't want anything but by now I know she has something for me. She is really caring so I am guessing, and I am little curious.

"I brought you my favourite novel. Me before you, I started to read when I had my breakup. It was messy but this book was my hope." She doesn't shows but even saying this hurts her. I don't want to ever hurt her.

"Hey, thats sweet Cookie. I will surely read and tell you. Lets go, we are almost near the gallery." I said and parked the car nearby the gallery.

We walked and she held my hands while walking, I can't say how much goodness and warmth it felt.

We came inside the gallery and she was so excited and looking at her I am excited.

We roamed around while holding hands and talked about the pieces of art. She thinks deep and I like how she sees the world.

We then decided to leave early since I wanted to take her to bandstand and drop her home.

We drove to Bandstand and walked on rocks, hand in hand.

We sat on a rock. She was siting close to me and we were looking at the sky.

She removed her earphones and asked if I wanna listen to it. I took the earphones and she started to play 'Sham Mastani' by Kishore Kumar.

We took a photo as well. We listened to songs for quite some time and it felt amazing. Like me, she always loves old songs, they are gems.

Then she kept her head on my shoulder, it felt so good. I can't even explain.

"You know, today was a dream and you can't imagine how hard you made me to make a choice. Today was definition of perfect. I never imagined a girl like me would ever have a date like this." She said as if she was sobbing.

"I am okay with whatever you choose, princess. I already made my decision. And you deserve so much more than this. If you let me, I want to be the person who makes you happy." I said and she was looking me in eye.

"You are very sweet Kanan, and as much as I want to, I can't give you happiness. I can't love again." She said in a sorry tone.

"Let me love you. You being here gives me happiness." I say and she smiles.

"We will see. Lets enjoy this moment before it becomes a memory. It feels so right." She says and keeps her head on my shoulder again.

We sat there for sometime in silence. But silence wasn't killing me, there was so much peace in the moment. I don't want it to end.

"Shall we leave? It's late. Even though I want to stay." She says.

"Stay forever. But right now let's go home. But there is one thing left." As soon as I finish she becomes happy.

We walk back to the car and then I drive to the cake shop.

"Give me a minute, I will be back." I say her and before she responds I leave.

I went in and asked for my order. The lady in the counter called manager.

"Hello sir, the order you placed was fallen on the ground. We are deeply sorry. We made cupcakes instead and this will be on the house." She said and I was bit angry.

"That works, thanks." I take and leave for car.

I got in car, and Cookie was suspicious.

"Here, it's for you. Open it." I tell her and she does what I said.

"Why thank you cupcakes? She asked me. I am glad she asked.

"Well because you agreed to coming on a date with me even when you didn't know if you wanted to or not. I am really happy, you gave me a chance. I am thankful. And i wanted you to know that I am extremely happy." I say and she hugs me.

"This is the best part of the best date ever. I don't know what to say. I mean I am glad I said yes to the date." I smiled as she completed her sentence and drove her back to her house.

We almost reached her house and I stopped the car.

"I don't want to pressure you in anyways. Take how much ever time you want to take, I am here. Today was definitely the best day of my life." I say and she gives me her brightest smiles.

"Today was my best day too. Thank you for everything. I will meet you tomorrow in college. Drive safe. Good night." She opens the door then.

"Good night Cookie." I smile and she leaves.

Today was so perfect. I wish Ma was here, so I could tell her I found her and went out with her.

Thank you so much for reading Let me know what you guys think of the date.

I am so so so so sorry about the late update. I have exams in a month.

I am so grateful for all my readers to wait for the chapter.

ALSO I HAVE AN ANNOUNCEMENT.

I HAVE AN INSTAGRAM ID FOR MY WATTPAD ACCOUNT

Instagram : @authoravanti

I will be uploading reels and spoilers there.

Do follow on instagram

Lots of love,

Avantika

Chapter 12

B usiness Deal

Avantika's POV :

He left and I got home. And well as soon as I entered, mom was in the dining area. I have no energy to fight with her today. So I quickly run towards my bedroom but she sees me.

"Where were you, if I may ask? Don't you see the time? And why are you so ready?" mom asks me and there were more questions but I cut her out.

"I was with a college friend. We went to mandir and then colaba. I got some books. I am sorry,Ma won't happen again." I say softly because I don't want to fight more. I am happy today after days, can't spoil my mood.

"Just few days until you would go off. Anyways be ready tomorrow. Don't go anywhere, tomorrow Chirag uncle and his family along with his son are coming officially. Behave with his son. His name is Dev Rawat. And if everything goes good, he will be our son in law." Ma dropped the bomb in front of me.

"Okay." I said and I left for my room

One moment I was happy. The other moment whole of my world was shattered. Today I finally felt like I was seen and heard and now all I know is I am a business deal and will be wedded off soon.

I always thought I was a burden to my family. They provided me with food, clothes and education. But they never talked to me in a loving way.

As I am a single child my parents never tried again because they were scared if it would be an unfortunate daughter again.

I got in a night suit and sat there for a moment.

I decided to look into today's day again. It started out unexpected and ended unexpected.

Kanan picked me. Usually I am the one who picks everyone but he picked me. That alone was enough to convince me to date him. He cares about his people a lot that is all I can say. And he knows how to treat his woman.

When Moksh and I went out for the first time, he was busy on his phone and then when we talked he gave me a list of behaviour I can't act. He said it would affect him as he is in college. He always wanted me to be dressed in a way I didn't like. Moksh ordered food for both and we ate. We didn't talk much. He just told me I was his girlfriend and I being unaware said yes. And then he dropped me. But before that he kissed me. It was the first kiss of my life. It was unexpected but it felt forced. I didn't like it, but when I told him I didn't like how he kissed me. He said fine he would never kiss me again. And I felt sorry so I kissed him, and he in his anger bit my lips, which was swollen for 4 days so he didn't meet me.

And I am lost in dark thoughts. But then my phone buzzed. It was a notification from Kanan. This guy makes me happy even just by his message, how do I tell him? That tomorrow morning I will commit to someone else for ever?

KS : I reached home. I had lot of fun. Thank you so much for saying yes for a date. It was perfect.

I read his text and I felt like crying. I wanted to tell him how much I wanna spend my life with him. He treated me better than my parents ever did.

Avantika : It was my pleasure Kanan. I just felt so lucky to go on a date with you. Thank you!!

I texted him and decided to take my journal out and started writing.

Dear Kanan,My life was full of downs before you entered. The day I met you for the movie, I had got the worst news of my life without even knowing the news or anything you made me happy. I didn't have to tell you to do something for me. I am used to telling people what they should do for me and rarely anyone turns up. I am used to that Kanan. Don't make me happy in the coming days. When all I know is I can't give you the happiness you deserve. I wish I could be the girl who could give you surprises and make you laugh always but tomorrow I am getting signed for someone else. If destiny played a miracle and I get a chance to be yours, I would do it. But I know my life. A girl like me who never had love of her family, you made her feel loved. If I could share my happiness for you, I would be ready to take any pain in the world. I know I am going to break your heart when you get to know about the arrangement. But I will try my to make you hate me. It's easy let other person hate you than have them waiting for you. For all you did for me today Kanan, I owe you so much. Thank you so much for doing it. You are very rare. I hope you know it.

I never would be brave enough to give it to him. So I decided to write it down. And I slept. It was a rough night. The nightmare appeared again and I woke up out of no where. I tried to be calm and saw it was almost 6:30 am. I decided to take a shower and get ready as the Rawat's would be here by 9:00 am.

I went in shower and took a bath.Then I decided a saree as Maa had decided to ask me to wear a saree.

I decided to go with a pink hand printed organza saree with a choker and open hair. I then did light make up.

I went in the hall to see the all all decked up. Mom and dad were also dressed up and were waiting for me.

As I walked near the mom an dad, dad started talking.

"Please do me a favour and make sure, Dev loves you when he sees you. It is very important for my deal. Don't talk with him because anything you speak would be stupid." He said and went to check the arrangements.

As soon as he left mom started.

"Do us a favour and get married to him. He will keep you happy and you anyways are nothing but useless. In this way atleast you will make your dad and me happy. Knowing we don't have to take care of you for a life time."

I was hurt, but I am used to having this conversations. I keep calm and sit at one place until the Rawat's arrive.

As soon as they arrived everyone was looking out for them and I was sent in kitchen to get them tea and coffee.

I slowly walked towards them and I didn't choose to look up. I kept the tray on the table and stood near mom, she was sitting.

"Let Dev and Avantika talk. And we all elders should talk about the business." Chirag uncle said and I smiled.

I didn't want this marriage to happen. Why is this happening? Krishna ji I know you do everything for a reason but this is not done right? I wanted to write a book. Make myself happy, I didn't want to be sold as a business deal.

I lead the way and Dev walked behind me. I didn't look at him till now. Is he not trying to understand I didn't want this?

We entered in my room and went in the balcony.

"So, what do you like to do?" He asked me to break the ice.

"I write and read. You?" I said in a humble tone.

"I work with my dad for his business. I like music. I love singing." He said and i sensed some irritation when he said dad's business.

"Do you want this?" He asked and I got confused.

"wha?" I ask to understand the context.

I looked at him when he answered. He was wearing a shirt and he looks handsome.

"The whole marriage?" He said and i had a question mark face.

"I don't want to answer anything that can hurt my dad's business." I say in a low voice.

"You do understand right that this is going to be lifetime? It's your life! He said in a concerning tone and the bubble around me bursted. I was sobbing.

"I never did anything for my parents. This is the only chance to make it right for them. I would not be a burden for you, don't worry." I said as I sobbed.

"Hey, I don't mind you being with me. But you can't be happy in a marriage without love. Just tell me you don't want this as much as I don't want it and we will figure a way out." He said and each word felt like a hug.

"What will we do?" I ask him

"I can convince my dad to not marry me to you, as I want to go to London for my studies. Till that time you can maybe find a job and move out?" He said in a questioning way.

"I am okay, lets just pretend right now. The talk went good and you can talk to your dad." I said and he smiled.

We went downstairs and everyone was talking about how mine and Dev's wedding would help the business. The families then left for their respective work after deciding to let me and Dev meet whenever we want.

This all was traumatising. I decided to take a walk in the park.

I didn't check the phone whole day, as I had no energy to see what is happening.

When i finally checked the phone I had 2 missed calls from Kanan, 5 missed calls from Cheryl.

And unlimited texts from both of them. I didn't have the courage to tell anyone about today.

I was keeping my phone, Kanan was calling me again. He deserves to know.

I picked up and said Hey.

"You are okay? Are you fine? I was worried. You didn't even come to college. Is everything okay?" He cares for me so much, every word he spoke had so much compassion.

"I am okay. I will tell you everything tomorrow. Could you please pick me.? I say in humble tone.

"Sure, Cookie."

We then talked for 2-3 minutes and then I cut the call.

He cares for me so much and I have no right to give him hope. Now that Dev is in the picture, it is wrong to hurt him. Hurting him hurts me I don't know why.

I got home and decided for tomorrow's outfit.

I then did some journalling and slept early. I wanted to go to college but before that I wanted to take kanan somewhere we can sit and talk.

I texted Kanan to pick me up at 7am.

Krishna ji please make sure everything goes okay and I don't hurt him, and if possible don't let me lose him.

Thank you so much for reading I am grateful for you.Let me know how you guys feel about this chapter □

Please VOTE, COMMENT and SHARE.

Follow me on Instagram: Authoravanti

I will be posting spoilers on Instagram and make sure you get the spoilers.

I am sorry for posting so irregular.

Lot's of love,Avanti

Chapter 13

She is mine.

Kanan's Pov :

Cookie asked me to pick her up at 7 am. She said she wanted to talk to me in private, I don't feel good about talks. It has always made me unhappy.

When I was 9 years old, dad said he wanted to talk to me about mom. She was admitted in hospital because she had an ache in her stomach. That's what dad told me, it was only after years I found out that she had cervix cancer. Since then I read everything about women's health, so some day if I have a wife and a daughter I would be able to take care of them. Dad told me mom had left us and went to a better place, she won't be coming back but she loves me a lot. I didn't take the news well back then, I cried for months and I missed her.

Dad and I never had a good relationship. He loved me but he was busy with business, mom and I were very close. But after mom died, dad and I grew closer. We become each other's support system. I started to learn about the business. It was good to bound with dad but I missed mom always.

She is and will be my angel of light.

I drove to Cookie's house, and I am honestly blank to what is to come.

She was standing near the corner I always pick her. She was looking so beautiful.

She got in the car.

"Good morning, Kanan. Thank you for picking me up in the morning." She said and I was busy staring at how effortlessly beautiful she was looking.

"Good morning, Cookie. Your welcome, I like picking you up. You look beautiful." I say and she smiles, though she looks tensed.

"Lets drive to a cafe, I want to talk to you about few things." This sounded serious and I did as she sad.

I drove to the cafe and we listened to some songs while driving. She played her favourite song.

The lyrics were so soothing.

Baaton ke matlab zaroori nahinHo labz ya lab zaroori nahinAankho hi aankho me ek dusre keHum aao na sapne salone sune..

Chup chaap baithe huye khwab haiBechain hai thode betab haiAndar kahin jo bhi selab haiJaatein karo baatein karo..

Baitho kabhi sath meri bhi doBaatein karo baatein karoChahe bhale baad me todd doVaade karo vaade karo!

It felt like she was trying to portray something or maybe she just likes the song and its good.

The drive was around 30-45 minutes. It was silent drive with lots of music.

We reached the cafe. I parked the car and got down to open the car door for her.

We went inside and there was a couple with a small baby. The baby was crying continuosly.

We got a table little far from the baby.

We ordered 2 latte and were sitting there.

Cookie was constantly looking at the baby.

"You should go and hold the baby." I suggested, she wanted to do it. I could see it in her eyes.

She nodded and started to walk in the direction of the baby.

She asked the lady, who was the mother if she could hold the baby and just stroll. The lady looked tired and agreed.

Cookie took the baby in her hand and she was looking so adorable with a baby. She started to stroll and slowly the baby started to calm down and eventually went to sleep.

Cookie returned to the table after giving the baby to the mother.

"You are going to be an amazing mother someday." As soon as I said this, cookie started crying.

She leaned into me while crying and I hugged her tight. It felt like she needed that hug more than anything. I didn't want to ask her what happened but I couldn't see her crying. Seeing her cry was so painful.

I gave her lots of hugs and she was slowly calmly down. I got her a glass of water and some chocolate, because crying is exhausting.

She calmed down and took deep breaths.

"Thank you for hugging me and not asking me questions." She said with her cute sobbing tone.

"It was my place to calm you down and you look really cute right now." I said and she blushed. She is so perfect.

We then drank some coffee and she was disturbed and I didn't want to force her into telling anything, she doesn't want to tell me.

"You wanted to talk? Are you okay?" I ask because I am impatient.

"Yes there are certain things we need to discuss before we get going with us." She said and I blushed. She told us. She is giving us a chance????

"Get your horses together, sweetheart".She said and laughed at me. She called me sweetheart too.

"Trying." I replied.

We were seated next to each other at the cafe. She was looking at me with love and care. And I was reciprocating.

"Let me tell you something you didn't know about me and you can tell me too?" I said and she nodded.

"I am a single child and I am a very shy person. I barely talk to people and especially girls are someone I can't talk to. You are an exception. I was 9 when my mom passed away. She had cervical cancer. She was one of the most friendly people ever. After her death dad and I got closer and we started to enjoy each other's company." I said and she was almost sobbing. She hugged me and I hugged her back. It was a wholesome moment.

" I am so sorry about your mom. And I am glad you and your dad bonded. I am lowkey happy you don't talk to girls." She said this and giggled.

"Your turn" I want to know about her.

"There is a lot, what do you want to know my dear?" She asked me and I am confused.

"Tell me something that I don't know but should know?" I say and she gets a little tense, so I hold her hand and she smiles.

"Before you, I had a boyfriend. We dated roughly for a year and he broke up. He was good, I don't know what else to say. We broke up 9 months ago. It was most painful at the last. His name was Moksh. We were in same school earlier. He was a brat, so was I. He is my biggest miracle and biggest problem." She said and I don't feel comfortable. I want to ask her why they broke up and she is okay? Was she hurt? She sounded painful while speaking about it.

"Okay, I don't know what to say." I said humbly and she held my hand tightly, felt like she was reassuraning me.

"You don't have to say anything. I can understand it is hard to accept a girl with a past. I don't blame you." She says and I hug her. Not Because I wanted to but because she is mine.

"It's not like that, baby. It's okay to have past. It's not okay to let your past stop you from living." I said and she smiled.

"There is something more I need to tell you." She said and I nodded.

"So my dad is a business man. He has a business partner who has a son. My dad wants me to marry him for the business. Like a business deal. I didn't come to college yesterday because they were visiting us. I met the son who was supposed to be my husband." She said this much and I got really uncomfortable.

"Then why I am here? Avantika? You started with mentioning about us. And now you are saying you are going to be someone's wife? What should I do?" I say in bit harsh tone.

"I am sorry, jaan. Just listen to me okay? I care for you. I connect with you. I want us as much as you want." She said while holding my hand.

She paused and took some breath.

"The guy himself doesn't wants this marriage. So we decided to tell his dad that he wants to go aboard to study and by that time I will earn and move out." She said in a reassuraning way.

"Okay. That's good. I mean I am glad you don't have to marry someone. By the way! What do you want to become, cookie?" I ask her and her eyes have sparkle.

"I want to be a writer. I want to write stories, experiences, blogs, and everything that makes one feel connected to me and themselves. I want to be a person who radiates happiness." She says with so much joy.

" I know you will become one. I hope I can be on the front row cheering you for the amazingly talented woman you are." I say and she blushes.

"Let's take a walk? And then I have something important to do." She says and we get out of the cafe.

"Okay, Cookie." I say and we then walk towards the car.

"So what do you think about love?" She asked me while walking.

"It's something that drives you to live your wildest and scariest dream. It's living miracle and agony. It's beautiful and ugly at the same time." I say and she smiles.

"I feel love is something that makes you happy when you are sad and sad when you are happy. It's the moments and the people who drive love. It's different for everyone and everything." She says and she smiles so beautiful.

We then walk for some time around the cafe and we hold hands while walking.

I saw a small boy selling flowers and she has that sparkle as we walk past him.

"Wait here, I will be back." I say her and leave to go get her flowers.

She didn't say she wanted flowers but ofcourse she will smile when I get her flowers. That's what maa told me, girls like the gesture rather than the thing.

I get her 3 roses and I walk towards her. She is smiling.

"Here, this is for you, cookie." I give her the roses and she hugs me.

"You didn't have to get me roses." She says and we'll that's lie. She is extremely happy I got her roses.

"Yes I didn't have to but I wanted to." I say and we come back to the car.

"You said, you wanted to meet someone?" I ask her.

"Yes, we are meeting the guy, who I was supposed to marry." As soon as she says this I make a grumpy, disgusting face. I don't like him okay!!!!

"Okay." I say plainly.

"I smell burning. Do you?" She asks to mock me. She knows.!

"Very funny, cookie." I say and she pouts.

We then drive to our college. The guy was supposed to meet us near college it self. Cookie told me she will get down and I will park the car and he back.

It took me some time to get the parking. I then went to find cookie. I saw her she was awkwardly hugging a guy and then it was obvious I got jealous.

I rushed in and hugged her.

"She is mine" I said to the guy and cookie was looking at me in shock.

"This is Dev, my dad's business partner's son." She says holding my hand tight.

"Hi, you must be Kanan. Avantika told me about you right now." Dev says and I am trying to smile.

"Yes. Hi. Nice to meet you." I shake hands with him.

"So, Avantika after lots of arguments my dad has decided to go with the business deal but without the marriage thing. So now you and I both are free. You can relax Kanan." He says and she smiles. Finally cookie is just mine.

"Thank you so much Dev!! It's been a pleasure." She says and shakes hands with him.

We then talk to each other for few minutes. Dev leaves and it's just me and cookie now.

"What are you doing tomorrow?" Cookie asks me.

"I am mostly free." I say her. I don't know why she wants to know if I am free or not.

" Good. Be ready at 8 am. I will pick you up." She says and I am dumbfounded.

"Okay. Where are we going?" I ask her. She refused to tell me.

"Should I be worried?" I ask to mock and irritate her.

" Yes" she says. She is difficult to irritate.

We then went to college and completed our lectures. Later we met post college. I asked if I could drop her and she denied. I am bit mad at her for denying but can't say anything because she is cookie. She can deny as much as she wants.

I then went out with Tej and Samay. We haven't played PS since so long. I was wanting to play with them since so long.

We had amazing matches, I won 5 out of 6 matches. Hehe, I had fun beating their asses after so long.

I told them about cookie. Like she is the girl I liked from the first day of college. They both were so shocked knowing I went on a date and didn't even tell them. I didn't tell them everything because it's us guys, we don't share everything like girls.

I then went home, had dinner with dad. And decided to watch some anime episodes.

It was quite late. I decided to sleep because tomorrow cookie is going to take me out. I am excited.

I figured that I will take out my clothes tomorrow morning it self. I need sleep badly. I texted her.

Kanan : Good night cookie. I am excited for tomorrow. Sleep well.

Cookie : I am excited too. Be ready on time. Good night!!

She immediately texted back. I slept post that.

Helloo,Thank you so much for reading □I am so grateful for you all.Do let me know how do you guys feel? Please comment your thoughts.You can all connect with me on my Instagram. Authoravanti

Follow me on Instagram for spoilers and updates.

Please vote, comment and share.

It is one of the lengthy chapters I wrote for the first time and I have a surprise for you all in the next one.

So make sure you follow me on Instagram and Wattpad for updates.

Again, thank you so much my readers

Lots of love,Avanti

Chapter 14

Will you be my partner?

Avantika's POV:

I asked Kanan to go out with me tomorrow. I want to make it special for him. He made me feel so special for the date. Even he deserves it

I haven't taught what would I want to, where do I want to take him but again that's a suspense for him and me.

I got home, I ditched kanan to drop me home. So I can think what should I get him.

I thought maybe I should get him a shirt but that would be too much. God why is so difficult to plan something for guys.

I saw my crochet tools. And it felt like a sign or help from god. Let me make him a broquet of flowers that are crocheted.

I started crochet and I got soo engrossed in doing it. It was late in night but I am almost done.

I write him a letter.

Dear Kanan,You are really special and a sweetheart. The way you treat me since day one is so perfect and I feel special whenever you treat me like this. I made this flowers for you, so they never die. I hope whenever you see them, you smile the hardest and remind yourself, how special you are. I hope you like the flowers□!!

I pack the flowers and the letter together. I haven't thought about what to do tomorrow but I know I will figure it out. I want to surprise him but it is so difficult to surprise him.

But I do have a plan. I am planning to take him for a food tour in the city. I know maybe he knows this place but exploring it together is going to be a great experience.

I am planning on taking the car, it's so hot out there and I am planning to drive. Let Kanan be the passenger princess.

I haven't decided on any outfit but I am gonna wear a cotton dress.

Tomorrow we are going to be a tourist in our own city and we will be looking for each other's beautiful hearts !

I finally decided to get some sleep, because I can't afford to look like a zombie, I am so tired.

After a lot of thoughts about tomorrow, I finally fell asleep.

It was approx 5:45 am, when I woke up. I then took a shower, and sat down to do light make up. It's so hot outside. I initially decided to take scooty but looking at the weather forecast I am gonna go take a car. I am planning to reach at his place early and then take him for a movie first. But first coffee.

I started Spotify and I started my favourite playlist that's full of Hindi songs. And as I started to get dressed the most apt song played, and I started smiling on it.

aaj kahenge dil ka fasaanajaan bhi lele chaahe zamaanaaaj kahenge dil ka fasaanajaan bhi lele chaahe zamaanamaut vahi jo duniya dekhemaut vahi jo duniya dekheghut ghut kar yoon marana kya

Then I dress into a cotton suit.

I dressed and I left for his house.

Avantika : Get ready, reaching your house in 20 minutes.

KS : What? Okay.

He immediately texted back. I know I know I said I will meet him at 8 am but I am too excited to meet him and he is already up. So I guess 20 minutes is a good time.I drive to his house listening to old hindi songs, they are so good. I am driving

I reached his house and I am waiting outside for my ...i mean..Kanan.

I call him and he picked up in panic, I have never called him in real life. I ask where is he? He said he is almost ready.

People say girls take time to get ready but in reality its the guy who takes hours to be on time.

I check shows on bookmyshow. I want to take him for movie because I want to.

I don't want to roam with him and have no where to go, I mean its peaceful to do nothing with him.

He finally comes , after making me wait for 5 minutes.

"I am so sorry to make you wait, you look beautiful." He says and I blush.

I know nothing is official but well he makes me blush.

"I am okay to wait for you. You look handsome." I say and he starts to touch my forehead, like he is checking temperature. I had a question mark on my face.

"You complimented me? Are you my cookie?" he says and I laugh.

"Haha, very funny." I say.

"So where are we going?" He asks he is a curious person.

"Breathe, check the cabinet opposite to you." As soon as I finish my sentence, he finds the flowers and the letter.

He started smiling even before he took out the flowers and letter. He looks so adorable right now. I just want him to smile like this always.

"Did you make this?" He asks me while I was driving.

"I know a bit of crochet, I thought to give you crochet flowers as they will never die and they may make you smile, an attempt to make you smile." I say and he looks at me with so much affection.

"Thank you so much cookie, this is very special to me. I will always keep them close to me. You know, I somehow always knew you were very talented. And I was right about it." He says and i touch his thighs as a token of agreement in my praise and I blushed.

"Okay, so I am bit confused. We can either go to movie or roam on streets." I ask in bit confusing tone.

"Lets go for movie." He says, somehow it feels like he always know what I want.

"Which movie" I ask him.

"Rocky and Rani ki Prem Kahani? Since its trending right now?" He asks me.

"Sounds good." I say and he starts to search.

"Take in Lower parel. I have a thing planned for afternoon." I say and he does exactly this.

"I see." He says and booked tickets for 8:30 am.

I then drive to lower parel, Palladium.

We parked the car and started walking inside the mall. It was kinda dark in the parking lot, so Kanan held my hands.

We started walking towards the PVR, and we were still holding hands, butterflies.

We then went inside the theatre and sat on our sits. He booked a couple seat, I guess or it's just my head telling me it's for couples.

"Do you want anything to munch?" He asked me.

"Do you? Fill your stomach little less, we are going to eat so much in afternoon." I say and he is confused but happy.

"I will get popcorn, and sit here only." I say and he frowns, because of course he wanted to go and get the food.

I go and get popcorn. And I have never been so excited about a movie.

If I am being honest, I am not excited about movie, I am excited to sit next to him for 3 hours.

I take the popcorn and go inside. He sees me and he smiles.

We started eating popcorn even before the movie started. We chatted a bit in between. He was curious about where we are going to go. I give him subtle hints but I don't tell him.

Then the movie started, the movie was a perfect option for us.

It was a perfect bend of old time romance and modern romance, we fit in both. Yes, Avantika you think of Kanan and you as we.

We watched the movie holding hands, and I even fed him popcorn and he blushed. He looks so cute when I feed him and he blushes.

Kanan loved the movie and got emotional when Rocky's grandpa died, seeing him even I got emotional. He then kept his hand on my arm and pulled me towards him. I leaned on and we watched rest of 20-25 minutes movie like that only.

"That was a good decision." He said and I smiled in agreement.

"I loved the movie." I said and held his hands. He is shy so my extrovert ass does it myself.

There were so many old songs in between movie, we both sang in between and I loved it.

"Now?" He asks me.

"We are going food hoping." I say and he squeals.

"I thought, best way to make you happy is to get you food." I say and he stops me and hugs me, I hug in back.

We then walked towards the car and I opened the door for him.

Then I drove to sion.

I stopped at legendary GURU KRIPA.

"Lets, make you eat some chole samosa and chole bhature with some rasmalai" I say and he smiles in his most perfect way.

We sat in AC because it was so hot outside, we ordered the food.

"So, How's your day going?" I ask him.

"Can't imagine anything better." He said.

"The is going to be more." I said

The food arrived till then.

"I can't wait, cookie." He smiled and his attention is shifted to food.

"Wait' I stopped him.

I took the fluffy bhature and made a small bite, dipped it in chole, added an onion ring, and the fed him.

OMG, HIS ACTUAL REACTION.

"This tasted even better with your hands." He said and I blushed this time.

We ate the food while chatting and feeding each other, in short we enjoyed food.

"This place has good food, I wish we could come here often." He says.

"We can, sweetheart." He held my hand as I said it.

"Well the shop, you see A-1 samosa, are famous for their variety of weird samosas, wanna try?" I ask him.

"Always." He said in enthusiasm.

We crossed the road, and bought 2 of their bestsellers.

"This is so good." He said while enjoying his bite.

"I am happy, to see you enjoy." I said and he blushed.

We then decided to go back to car, and I wanted to take him to Matunga, so we drove there.

We went to the back side of five garden, and I parked the car.

We both got down and walked to a small cart selling sandwiches, we ordered one sandwich. There were 2 carts more, one selling beverages and other selling chat items.

We ordered a cold coffee and ate panipuri till the sandwich was getting toasted.

Then the sandwich came, he was holding cold coffee in one hand and sandwich plate in another, so I decided to make him bite the sandwich. He makes so cute faces when he eats something food.

Seeing him happy made me realise, I made a good decision.

We enjoyed our cold coffee and sandwich and then decided to walk a bit in the garden, while holding hands.

We walked for around 40-50 minutes and we had our earphones , so we jammed on some songs.

We then headed back to car.

"Now, madam?" He knows there is more, smart ass.

"Well it is all incomplete without bandstand." I say and he smiles.

It was 30 minutes drive. We chatted a bit in general. He was telling me he told Samay and Tej. I am yet to tell Cheryl about today.

We reached our favourite spot and we were just in time for sunset.

We sat next to each other and my head was on his shoulders.

"I need to tell you something." I say after we sat there for a while. The feeling of keeping my head on his shoulders never gets old. I love the feeling.

He gets alert and looks at me like I have his whole attention.

"I like this. It feels perfect. I know I am not perfect. I have many flaws, but when I am next to you I don't care. I feel happy. When I see you smile I am just happy from my heart. I had stopped living ever since you came, I haven't stopped living. I know we haven't had lot of time together but I want to spend time with you. I want this. I want to spend my happy and sad moments with you. I want to be the person who makes you happy. I want to be the shoulder who is there when you need. I want to learn about you. I want to be with you in this journey. I want to be the Avantika who knows she is Kanan's cookie." I say this with a little sobs in my eyes.

Kanan was already emotional and happy.

I get on one knee and remove a rose crochet.

"WILL YOU BE MY PARTNER?" I ask him while I am on one knee.

He gets down on his knees and takes the flower, while he is smiling.

"I would be mad if I said NO to a girl like AVANTIKA SHAH." He said and we hugged.

We hugged like no one saw us, we didn't care.

This was all it.

The answers to my prayers. My home.

The feeling he got me. The way he makes me feel.

After a while we stopped hugging and he made his face come closer to my head and he stopped before he touched my head.

"Can I kiss your forehead?" He asked me and I gestured yes.

He kissed my forehead and in that moment I was happiest girl, the simple fact he asked for concern before kissing my forehead.

We then got up.

All the people around us started to smile. One of the other couples, was kind enough and they took some photos. We imported the photos and kanan and I stayed there for a while soaking everything.

We then walked and we were holding hands, looking at each other and smiling.

We went back to the car, and he insisted on driving but I made a baby face so let me drive.

"So, how do you feel?" I ask him while driving.

"Unbelievable. I am yours and you are mine, cookie." He says with so much love.

"I sure am." I say with same amount of love.

"There is so much I want to know about you, but don't ever think you have to tell me with force. I can wait for you for as long as you want me to. I am okay with you telling me everything late but I am not okay with you being uncomfortable for even a minute." He says and I want to sob so bad. He is so adorable.

"Thank you so much for being so understandable." I say and he taps on my back.

Next 10-15 minutes we didn't talk much but it was so peaceful.

We almost had reached Kanan's house.

"So, I guess we need to call it a day?" I say with a hint of sadness in my voice.

"Yes, we need to call it a day to this wonderful 1st August. A day when I got girl of my dream. We can always create more memories, don't be sad cookie." He reassures me even without me telling him anything.

"You na" I lose my seat belt and kiss him on forehead. He smiles so hard and blushes even harder.

"You are very sweet. I am lucky to be your girlfriend." I say and he blushes on the word girlfriend.

"I am more lucky, to be the boyfriend of the prettiest girl." He knows how to make me blush.

He then kissed my forehead and said me bye.

"Text me once you reach home. Drive safely cookie." He says with concern.

"I will for sure. Bye sweetheart." I say and he responds immediately.

"Bye cookie, take care. Thank you for today." He says and I smile.

I drive back to my house.

Thank you so much for reading

I know, I updated super late and I am really very sorry for that, I have my exams going on and hence was not able to write. I have received so much love, so beautiful reviews that made me smile. You guys are the cutest. I am so grateful for all the time, love and positivity you guys give me. LET ME KNOW HOW YOU GUYS FELT ABOUT THIS CHAPTER!!. I cried writing certain parts of the chapter. This was a surprise, be ready for the cute college romance.

PLEASE VOTE COMMENT AND SHARE.

Follow me on Instagram : Authoravanti

Currently we are doing #navratriwithkantika on Instagram.

Thank you so much guys for everything.

Also, the places mentioned in the story are real places, you guys can visit them if you stay in Mumbai or are planning to visit Mumbai.

Lots of love,Avantika

Chapter 15

College Romance

Kanan's Pov :

She just dropped me and I kissed her forehead, prior to that she kissed my forehead. She got me flowers and a handwritten note, a food hopping date, a movie outing, and the proposal at the bandstand! Thats a lot to absorb in my defence.

This day seems unreal. She is my cookie now, well she was now just she knows. Hehe.

The AVANTIKA SHAH is my girlfriend.

I am dancing and screaming and what not.

I read her note around 100 times already and it still makes me have those butterflies.

I changed and went to have dinner with dad. Even he asked what's up with me, I just said so things. He would be the happiest to meet cookie but I am not sure if cookie wants to tell or not so I will keep that decision for her to make.

I quickly completed my dinner and cookie had already texted.

Cookie : I reached home, I will talk to you around 9:45 pm?

KS : Hello, I had so much fun! You are literally the best.

It was already 9:40 pm so I waited a bit for her text and then started the zone of texting.

Cookie : Me too, jaan. So did you have dinner?

KS: Yes just now. Did you cookie?

Cookie : Yes. I want to ask you something.

KS : You should never ask me about anything. I am yours, you can ask me anything at any time.

Cookie : You are really sweet. I wanted to post today's photos. Should I?

KS: Do you want me to post and you repost?

Cookie: You would do that really?

KS: Ofc, cookie. Tomorrow morning we will select on the way to college?

Cookie: Sure. Will you pick me up?

KS: I would be honoured. Just one more question.

Cookie: Go on.

KS: By any chance do you be interested in going to garba with me?

Cookie: You kidding me? I would be honoured. But do you know garba? Since you know you are Punjabi.

KS: Don't worry about it. Good night Cookie. Take care princess.

Cookie: Good night sweetheart.

I can't believe still. I started to search about garba classes. I want to be able to dance with her. It's obvious she loves garba and it's my duty to make her have fun.

I sleep like a baby and I am not been so happy ever since mom left.

I didn't realise when I slept but I when I woke up it was almost as if, I sleep another second and I am gonna be very late.

I quickly got dressed and skipped breakfast as I want to do that with cookie.

God I miss her so much.

I drive to her place and call her. She said she will take another 5 minutes so I start radio till then and my new favourite song starts playing.

Tere bin nahin lagta mera dil Tere bin nahin lagta mera dil Tere bin nahin lagta mera dil Ab mujhse aa mil

Kaise in lamhon ki yaadon ko Pal mein hi main tham lun Tere hi khwabon mein rehti hun Har pal hai tujh mein sukun (sukun) Dil bhi aawaara hai Tujhpe sab haara hai Tujh mein hi khone lagi hun ab teri baatein karun

As soon as cookie entered this lyrics started playing.

Channa ve hun kol baija aakeYun door na tu jaa ve Sanu eida na tadpa veTere bin nahi lagta mera dil Tu hi rab hai tu hi mera saahilSun sajna mujhse tu aa mil Ab to tu aa mil aa mil

She hugged me while she sat in her place, and I hugged her back. She smells like strawberries and vanilla.

"Good morning cookie. You look so pretty." I say and she blushes. How can I ever get over this.

"Good morning Jaan. You look handsome. I am hungry" she says in her cute baby voice and my heart melts.

"So, I am hungry." She said and well i am happy cause I was just taking her to have breakfast.

"I just know a place." I say and she gives me her cutest smile.

I drive to a small stall which sells South Indian breakfast and as soon as I drive there she just gives me her biggest smile.

I get down and open door for my princess.

She holds my hand and we walk towards the stall.

The vendor asks us what we want and I order plain dosa and combined medu vada and idly.

"How do you know what I want?" She asks me with curiosity.

"I don't know what you want always but I always try to know what you need right now to make you happy. A happy cookie means happy Kanan." She laughs and gives me a cheek kiss.

I am literally melting to her kiss, she is purest of all.

We then had our breakfast and I want my every breakfast with her.

Then we drive to the college and we sit together along with our gang in the last benches.

I was holding her hand throughout.And while we were writing she wrote me cute notes in her book and I replied to her cute notes in her book.

And our friends cringed and laughed but well they deserved to do it.

After the lectures we all went to canteen for the most important discussion.

We were sitting in canteen and cookie started talking.

"GUYS, NAVRATRI IS STARTING FROM TOMORROW AND WE ARE GONNA PLAY ALL THE 10 NIGHTS! NO EXCUSES FROM ANYONE." she said bold and clear and she looked like if we deny she would hit us but cutely.

"COOKIE, we will match our outfits" I say and she looks like something hit her unexpected.

"Really? That's soo cute. OMG! You are the best." She says and well she started her garba from her itself.

I then sit and see her in aw of her cuteness and finally it's the time I Hate. I have to drop her!

I dropped her and went for my garba classes.

The guy who was teaching garba promised he would make me learn in 6 hours everything.

I went for garba and returned late all exhausted.

I had 3 missed calls from cookie while I was getting fresh.

I call her.

———————————————————

www.ingramcontent.com/pod-product-compliance
Lightning Source LLC
Chambersburg PA
CBHW070409200726
48294CB00003B/1143